Ellie's Fun Day at the Farm

Coauthor Elle Fair
Coauthor Marci Fair
Photographer Courtney Fair
Assistant Editor Chloe Fair
Cover & Layout Designer Nelly Murariu

We have always loved visiting
and meeting new animals.
We have seen animals at the zoo,
so we decided to visit animals
living on a farm. We wanted to
share our adventure and
hope you will want
to visit the animals
like we did!

Elle Fair,
age twelve

Ellie and Pudgy were eating lunch. They wondered, "Where does our yummy food come from?" They had heard of farmers and their gardens and animals, but they had never been to a farm.

4

They decided to learn how farmers take care of so many animals and grow many foods we eat.

The first thing they saw at the
farm was a bright red tractor.
"*Hay,* this looks like fun!"

Ellie and Pudgy sat in the driver's seat. The tractor was huge and so were its wheels.

Ellie and Pudgy found one of their favorite things—a swing that looked like a horse. They raced Tommy the turtle to the swing, but he was very slow.

Then Spots the bunny bounced by to say hello. Spots invited Ellie and Pudgy to *hop* on over to meet her friend Baa the sheep.

9

The sheep liked to be together and play follow the leader. When one of them walked away, everyone else followed.

The sheep told Ellie to come *baa-ck* to play soon.

Fanny the Jersey cow said she makes the milk that they drink. They told her thank you, and then it was time to *moo-ve* it, *moo-ve* it to go meet the ducks.

Ellie and Pudgy walked to the lake. The ducks liked to drink water, search for food, and waddle around together.

Greg the goose waved his wings
to cool off and splashed everyone
nearby. Ellie told Pudgy, "The ducks
quack me up!"

Then they found
an *egg-stra* special
surprise—hidden
duck eggs!
Pudgy carefully
sat on them to try
to keep them warm.

13

More goats came by, nibbling on grass and their feed. They told Ellie they make milk, which is made into cheese.

Gabby the curious goat
said hello to Pudgy
and introduced her to
her *maaaa-maaa*.

The happy goats were *kidding* around as they played and ran in the yard.

16

Baby the goat
was hungry, so
Ellie fed her with
a bottle. "What a
sweet *baa-by*,"
thought Ellie.

17

The goats were funny, and so was Miss Piggy the pig.
She greeted Pudgy first, and then she said hello to Ellie.

Miss Piggy asked if they wanted to roll around and play in the mud with her. She said, "*Oink* you glad you met messy me?"

19

Nearby, Rudy the rooster
asked Holly the red hen,
"Why are an elephant and
a penguin at the farm?"

20

Rudy asked Ellie and Pudgy
"*Cock-a-doodle-do!*
Are you from the zoo?"

"Oh no," said Ellie. "We are
making new farm friends
and counting eggs, too!"

21

The baby chicks in the henhouse peeped,
"We jumped out of our eggs!"

Rudy the rooster said, "*Cluck cluck, maybe you can go find some food at the garden potluck!*"

23

So Ellie
and Pudgy
went to the
farmer's
garden in
search of
a snack.

24

They had not seen any butterflies at the beach "un-butterfly garden," but they found some beautiful painted ones here.

Ellie also found a pig that wanted to fly.

Pudgy found sunflowers as big as she was!

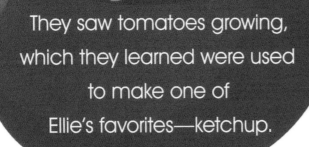

They saw tomatoes growing, which they learned were used to make one of Ellie's favorites—ketchup.

They found a shovel for digging. Miss Piggy would have loved to use it to help them play in the dirt.

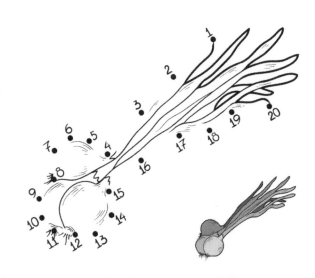

Pudgy told Ellie,
"*Lettuce* go see more!"
Ellie replied, "You seem
to like *corny* jokes!"

27

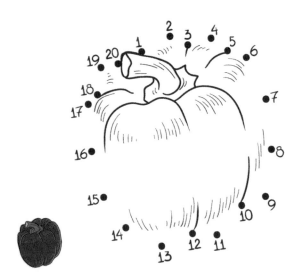

2
1
3
19 20
4
5
18
6
17
7
16
8
15
9
14
10
13
12
11

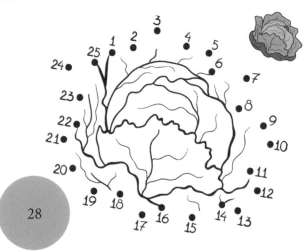

They saw onions,
rhubarb, and
red peppers
also growing in the garden.

3
25 1 2
4
24
5
23
6
22
7
21
8
20
9
10
19 18
11
17 16 15
12
14 13

28

After walking through the colorful garden, they relaxed on a swing that was just the right size. It would be snack time soon!

Ellie went to the stable next and met sweet Grits the horse. Grits said hi, then told her to visit Thunder, her *neigh-bor*.

They rode on friendly Thunder the
horse as he nibbled on the grass.
They imagined what it would be like
to be cowgirls and cowboys!

Sunshine the happy donkey lived around the corner.

She was
excited to
welcome
them.

She snuggled
with Ellie
and Pudgy
and said,
"*Hee-haw*, it is
so much fun to
play with you at
the farm!"

The farm was a fun place, full of friendly animals and yummy food.

Ellie and Pudgy enjoyed a farm-fresh snack of goat cheese, wheat crackers, and farm treats that tasted so good.

34

After their busy day, they rested on a hammock
and dreamed about the next adventure they would share.

Right before Ellie fell asleep,
she whispered to Pudgy,
"We have *goat* to come back!"

Games Ellie loves to play!

Fill in the crossword puzzle.

1. Cat 2. Cow 3. Duck 4. Chicken
5. Goat 6. Rooster 7. Turkey 8. Horse
9. Pig 10. Dog 11. Sheep

Answer: COUNTRYSIDE

Invite a friend to play a game!

?
FIND
10
DIFFERENCES

SHARE YOUR FAVORITE STUFFED

1

Set up your
favorite stuffed animals while
visting an animal farm.

2

Take a photo or
ask someone to help
you take one.

WE WILL RECOGNIZE YOUR CREATIVITY AND WILL LOVE

Animal Friends Too!

Here's how in four easy steps:

3

Upload and share your photo on our page, Facebook.com/ellieandpudgy

4

Tell us their names and type hashtag #elliesfriends

MEETING YOUR FAVORITE STUFFED ANIMAL FRIENDS TOO!

Dear Parents,

Children love animals and food, so visiting a farm seemed like the perfect fifth adventure! We hope that you enjoyed meeting these sweet animals as much as we did. We would like to say a special thank you to our dear friends Kevin and Lynn Kaley for sharing their family farm, Dobber's Pond and Farmette, with us. We also appreciate *Rancho Alegre Farm* for letting us come visit and make new animal friends!

Marci and Elle
#elliesfriends

www.ranchoalegrefarm.com

The Amazing Adventures of Ellie The Elephant:
Ellie's Fun Day at the Farm

Copyright ©2016 Marci Fair, Pacochel Press LLC
All rights reserved.
First Edition

Printed in the United States of America

Permission to reproduce or transmit in any form or by any means—electronic or mechanical, including photocopying and recording—or by any information storage and retrieval system, must be obtained by contacting the author by email at info@guiltfreemom.com.

Ordering Information
For additional copies contact your favorite bookstore, online store, or email info@guiltfreemom.com.
Special offers for large orders are available.

ISBN-10: 0-9963635-3-X
ISBN-13: 978-0-9963635-3-2

More of Ellie's Amazing Adventures Coming Soon!

www.EllieAdventures.com